D1271442

#8

BLACKOUT!

MARVEL

Spotlight

ABDOPUBLISHING.COM

Reinforced library bound edition published in 2018 by Spotlight,
a division of ABDO, PO Box 398166, Minneapolis, Minnesota 55439.
Spotlight produces high-quality reinforced library bound editions for
schools and libraries. Published by agreement with Marvel Characters, Inc.

Printed in the United States of America, North Mankato, Minnesota.
092017
012018

PUBLISHER'S CATALOGING-IN-PUBLICATION DATA

Names: Thompson, Robbie, author. | Stockman, Nathan; Campbell, Jim, illustrators.
Title: Spidey #8: Blackout! / by Robbie Thompson; illustrated by Nathan Stockman and Jim Campbell.
Other titles: Blackout!
Description: Minneapolis, MN : Spotlight, 2018 | Series: Spidey Set 2
Summary: When Peter's movie night with Gwen is interrupted by a citywide blackout, Spidey goes to investigate a mysterious noise and comes face-to-face with Electro.
Identifiers: LCCN 2017941925 | ISBN 9781532141560 (lib. bdg.)
Subjects: LCSH: Spider-Man (fictitious character)--Juvenile fiction. | Super heroes--Juvenile fiction. | Graphic Novels--Juvenile fiction.
Classification: DDC 741.5--dc23
LC record available at http://lccn.loc.gov/2017941925

Spotlight

A Division of ABDO
abdopublishing.com

ORIGIN ART BY NICK BRADSHAW & JIM CAMPBELL.

I KNOW WHAT YOU'RE THINKING.
BUT THIS *ISN'T* A DATE.
RAIDERS OF THE LOST ARK
MOJO MOVIES
CLASSICS MONTH
RAIDERS OF THE LOST ARK
ONLY REASON A GEEK LIKE ME EVEN *KNOWS* GWEN STACY IS BECAUSE WE TUTOR EACH OTHER FOR SCHOOL.
I WISH THEY'D MAKE ONE OF THESE MOVIES SET IN NEW YORK. THERE'S SO MANY ARCHAEOLOGICAL ADVENTURES TO BE HAD RIGHT *HERE!*
MOJO MOVIES
DIT.CO.
I MEAN, WE'RE STANDING ON TOP OF MILES AND MILES OF TUNNELS--WHO KNOWS WHAT'S DOWN THERE! DINOSAURS? BURIED TREASURE? ALIENS?
THAT RIGHT THERE IS WHY YOU'RE AN AWESOME HISTORY TUTOR.

YEAH, WELL, IT TAKES TWO TO TANGO.
THIS *ISN'T* A DATE.
RIGHT?

THIS MAY, OR MAY NOT, BE MY SEVENTH TIME SEEING THIS MOVIE.
HAH--ME, TOO!
SAW IT *TWICE* WITH FLASH.
=SIGH= FLASH THOMPSON. HER POTENTIAL BOYFRIEND.
DEFINITELY NOT A DATE.
HOW *ARE* THINGS GOING WITH FLASH?
FINE.
WE'RE JUST FRIENDS.
WAIT, WHAT--
KZZT

UM, IS IT ME, OR DID THE LIGHTS JUST GO OUT...?
I'M SURE EVERYTHING'S FINE--
--AH!
YOU KNOW WHAT? I'LL JUST GO CHECK.
BACK IN TWO SHAKES...

OKAY, THIS IS A PROBLEM.
BEEEP
HONK

BUT, IF I MAY ASK: HOW *BIG* A PROBLEM?
'CAUSE I MAY, OR MAY NOT, BE ON A DATE.

I JUST *HAD* TO ASK...
BLACKOUT!
ROBBIE THOMPSON writer
NATHAN STOCKMAN artist
JIM CAMPBELL colors
VC's TRAVIS LANHAM lettering
KHARY RANDOLPH & EMILIO LOPEZ cover
DARREN SHAN editor
NICK LOWE executive editor
AXEL ALONSO editor in chief
JOE QUESADA chief creative officer
DAN BUCKLEY publisher

COULD JUST BE A POWER OUTAGE.
THAT'S A THING THAT HAPPENS.
BUT THAT WOULDN'T SET OFF MY SPIDEY SENSE...
C'MON, FOCUS, PETER...
AH, THERE YOU ARE. TOUGH TO FIND A SPIDER...

...IN ALL THIS DARKNESS.
ELECTRO.
I REALLY SHOULD HAVE PUT THAT TOGETHER SOONER.

HEY, SPARKLES. LONG TIME.
YOU REALLY WANT TO TANGLE AGAIN?
"IT USUALLY DOESN'T END WELL FOR YOU...
"...PLUS, SINCE WE LAST WENT AT IT?
"I'VE MADE A FEW *ADJUSTMENTS*.
"WHICH IS GOOD FOR ME..."
...*BAD* FOR YOU.
BRAVO, SPIDER.
BUT AS YOU'RE ABOUT TO SEE...

...I'VE MADE SOME ADJUSTMENTS AS WELL!
GHHAHHHH!
...THAT JOLT...
...WENT THROUGH THE GROUNDING IN MY WEBBING... AND MY SUIT...
TONIGHT WILL BE OUR LAST ENCOUNTER, SPIDER. TONIGHT THE WORLD SEES YOU FOR WHAT YOU REALLY ARE: NOTHING.
WHAM
...CAN'T FEEL MY...
...ANYTHING...

I'VE TAKEN ALL THE ELECTRICITY IN MANHATTAN, SPIDER.
KABOOM

SAVED IT ALL UP *JUST* FOR YOU.
TONIGHT, YOU *DIE!*

DAILY BUGLE
NEW YORK'S FINEST DAILY PAPER
KRAK
IS THIS BECAUSE I KEEP STOPPING YOU FROM BEING A CROOK?
'CAUSE A SIMPLE THANK-YOU CARD WOULD SUFFICE.
OH, NO-- THAT SIGN!

PETER...? PETER...?!
BOOM

OH, NO!
DAILY BUGLE
NEW YORK'S FINEST DAILY

AH!

YOU OKAY?
I WAS UNTIL YOU *TACKLED* ME.

YOU'RE WELCOME...?
DON'T WORRY, I GET THAT ALL THE TIME.

WHOA. HEY.
HEY. NICE TO SEE YOU AGAIN.
YOU REMEMBER ME?
WHO COULD FORGET YOU?
LISTEN, I APPRECIATE THE HELP, BUT THERE'S A HOMICIDAL-SLASH-ELECTRICAL MANIAC ON THE LOOSE, SO--
BUT I CAN'T FIND MY FRIEND, PETER.
"FRIEND," HUH?
DEFINITELY. NOT. A. DATE.
DON'T WORRY--YOUR FRIEND, IS UH, ACTUALLY HELPING THE POLICE GET PEOPLE INSIDE.
WHAT, WHERE...?
HE'S, UH...RIGHT THERE.
YOU CAN'T SEE 'CAUSE IT'S TOO DARK BUT HE'S THE REAL MVP OKAY GREAT SEEING YOU AGAIN GOTTA GO!
PETER'S AN AWESOME GUY, BY THE WAY. FIRM HANDSHAKE. GREAT HAIR.
OKAY, BYE AGAIN!

YOU DONE PLAYIN' HERO, CHUMP?
C'MON, SPARKLES. LET'S NOT DO THIS.
WHATEVER IT IS THAT WE'RE DOING.
IT'S CALLED BEATING YOU DOWN, GENIUS.
OKAY, GOTTA GET THIS DUMMY AWAY FROM ACTUAL HUMANS.
IF ONLY WE WEREN'T FIGHTING IN THE MOST POPULATED CITY IN THE WORLD...
GAH!

OOOF!
...MUST BE SOME KINDA BLACKOUT...
...GUESS I'M WALKING...
...GONNA BE LATE FOR THE SHOW...
DOES EVERYONE ELSE SEE STARS RIGHT NOW, OR IS IT JUST ME?

IT'S JUST ME.

WAITASEC.
Subway
I KNOW A PLACE WHERE THERE'S NOBODY.
GWEN, YOU'RE A GENIUS.

SORRY, FOLKS, COMING THROUGH!
AIEEE!
WHAA--!

PLEASE DON'T LET THERE BE A LIGHT AT THE END OF THIS TUNNEL...

YOU THINK YOU CAN HIDE FROM *ME?!*

HIDE FROM YOU?
DON'T BE SILLY.
I'M GONNA NEED YOUR LIGHT.

IT'S DARK DOWN HERE!

DEAD END, SPIDER.
DON'T SAY IT.
DUDE.

YOU'RE TRAPPED.
YOU'RE RIGHT.
BUT SO ARE YOU.

BZZZT
TOOK ALL YOUR JUICE JUST TO FOLLOW ME DOWN HERE...

...DOWN HERE, WHERE THERE'S NO PEOPLE...AND MORE IMPORTANTLY...
...NO ELECTRICITY.
WHICH MEANS...
DON'T SAY IT.

LIGHTS-OUT!
DUDE.

SEE YA AROUND, SPARKLES.
YOU'LL PAY FOR THIS!
HE *SHOULD* PAY FOR THIS--*THE BUGLE* IS RIGHT: YOU'RE A MENACE!
UM...YOU'RE WELCOME...?
SIGH.
ALL RIGHT. BACK TO MY "NOT DATE."
IF I CAN FIND GWEN AT ALL.
PETER, THERE YOU ARE!

YOU OKAY?
YEAH, YOU?
YEAH! I MET SPIDER-MAN!

ME TOO. GREAT GUY. FIRM HANDSHAKE. HE SAID YOU WERE HELPING PEOPLE.

JUST DOING MY PART.
WELL, WHAT YOU DID WAS PRETTY COOL. *UM*, WHAT YOU DID THAT I DIDN'T SEE AT ALL--
Y'KNOW WHAT? I DON'T THINK THE POWER'S COMING BACK ON FOR A WHILE AND IT'S GETTING PRETTY LATE.
RAIN CHECK ON THE MOVIE?
SURE.
IT'S A DATE.

PRETTY SURE THEY'RE NOT GONNA LET YOU WEAR THAT GETUP IN JAIL, PAL.
NYPD
HEY, WHAT THE HECK IS--
BOOOM
WHAT THE...

YOU?!
NOW WHY WOULD YOU HELP ME?
I HAVE A PLAN TO DESTROY SPIDER-MAN, AND I NEED YOUR HELP, ELECTRO.
WHAT KIND OF PLAN?
WELL, TO BE FRANK, IT'S RATHER...

...SINISTER.
TO BE CONTINUED!

COLLECT THEM ALL!

Set of 6 Hardcover Books ISBN: 978-1-5321-4154-6

Hardcover Book ISBN
978-1-5321-4155-3

Hardcover Book ISBN
978-1-5321-4156-0

Hardcover Book ISBN
978-1-5321-4157-7

Hardcover Book ISBN
978-1-5321-4158-4

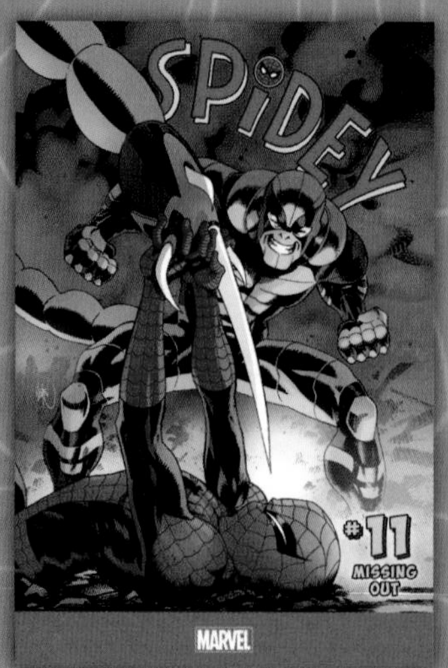

Hardcover Book ISBN
978-1-5321-4159-1

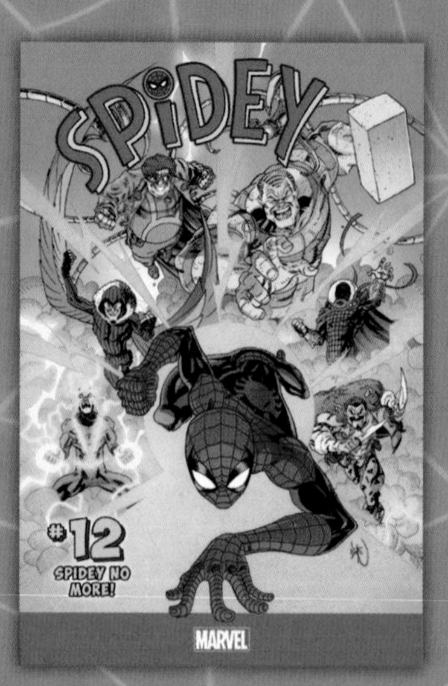

Hardcover Book ISBN
978-1-5321-4160-7